ON
Meadowview
Street

Henry Cole

Greenwillow Books
An Imprint of HarperCollinsPublishers

It was a big day. Caroline and her family were moving into their new house on Meadowview Street.

MEADOWVIEW ST.

After things were unpacked, Caroline's dad decided the grass was too tall and got busy mowing the lawn. Caroline was about to explore the new street to see if there *was* a meadow on Meadowview Street when she noticed a small blossom.

It's beautiful! Caroline said to herself. *And all alone.*

The mower was getting closer. Caroline thought, *I'd better do something quick!*

The mower came to a halt. "Daddy!" Caroline pleaded. "Couldn't you mow around my flower?"

"Hmph," he said, thinking, *Well, that's less mowing for me!*

Caroline raced inside the house.

She poked around the
boxes in the basement.

"Aha!" She smiled. "Some string and some sticks. Just what I need."

Before long, Caroline had made a small wildflower preserve.

Then she noticed another
flower had bloomed nearby.

Her preserve got bigger.

And bigger.

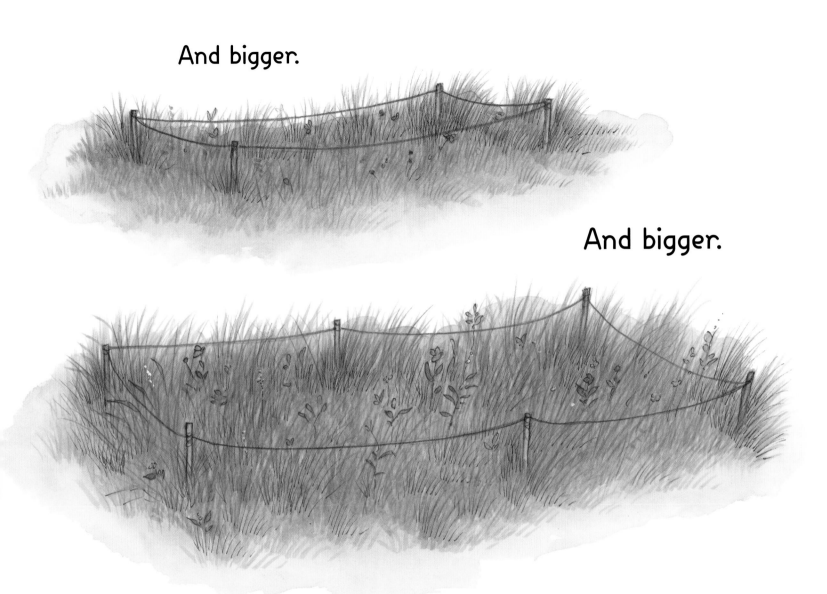

And bigger.

That butterfly seems to like my little garden, Caroline thought happily.

As the grass grew taller, more flowers popped up all over the yard.
Soon there were different kinds, in different colors, everywhere.

Caroline's dad had a great idea for the mower.

One day Caroline sat in her preserve, in the heat
of the sun. "My garden needs a shady spot," she said
to her parents.

"A shady spot sounds nice," replied Caroline's mom.

Soon a truck made a delivery. Caroline's mom took pictures.

"Welcome to your new home," said Caroline to the maple tree.

The next day, as Caroline admired the
maple tree, a wren landed on the end of
her shovel. "Oh! You're looking for a home,
too!" said Caroline.

Caroline and her dad got to work. They found some plans for building birdhouses. Caroline helped cut the wood and nail the pieces together.

Perfect! thought Caroline.
So did the wren.

In no time there were birds and insects everywhere,
around the tree and zipping among the flowers.
Soon the wren house was full of twigs for a nest.
Caroline wanted one more thing. "We need a place
where everyone can get a drink of water," she said.

The next day she and her dad began building a pond.

They dug a large, shallow hole and lined it with a heavy plastic sheet.
Caroline added plants that like living in water. She lugged large rocks
to the edge, making ledges and little caverns for creatures to live in.

The more Caroline and her family worked on their yard,
the more it changed. It was now a home to many things.

And soon, the Jacksons' yard changed.
And the Smiths'. And the Sotos'.

ladybird beetle

Now there really *was* a meadow
on Meadowview Street . . .

salamander

swallow

monarch caterpillars
on milkweed leaf

bee

mud turtle

coneflower

beetle

brown bat

dragonfly

meadow mouse

hummingbird

house wren

skink

wolf spider

black-eyed Susan

green snake

mallow

Small Copper butterfly
on bee balm

. . . and a home for everyone.

For C. W. R., with love

Acrylic paints were used to prepare the full-color art.
The text type is 17-point Dixon Medium.

Library of Congress Cataloging-in-Publication Data
Cole, Henry, (date).
On Meadowview Street / Henry Cole.
p. cm.
"Greenwillow Books"
Summary: Upon moving to a new house, young Caroline and her parents encourage
wildflowers to grow and birds and animals to stay in their yard,
which soon has the whole suburban street living up to its name.
ISBN-13: 978-0-06-056481-0 (trade bdg.) ISBN-10: 0-06-056481-4 (trade bdg.)
ISBN-13: 978-0-06-056482-7 (lib. bdg.) ISBN-10: 0-06-056482-2 (lib. bdg.)
[1. Nature—Fiction. 2. Lawns—Fiction. 3. Meadows—Fiction. 4. Suburban life—Fiction.] I. Title.
PZ7.C673450qm 2007 [E]—dc22 2006023761

First Edition 14 15 SCP 20 19 18 17

Greenwillow Books